≠
W938no

ALSO BY PATRICIA WRIGHTSON

THE ICE IS COMING
THE DARK BRIGHT WATER
JOURNEY BEHIND THE WIND
A LITTLE FEAR

(Margaret K. McElderry Books)

Night
Outside

Night
Outside

Patricia Wrightson

illustrated by Beth Peck

A MARGARET K. MC ELDERRY BOOK
ATHENEUM   1985   NEW YORK

Library of Congress Cataloging-in-Publication Data

Wrightson, Patricia.
Night outside.

"A Margaret K. McElderry book."
Summary: Two children in search of their pet
budgerigar meet the unusual people of the streets and
of the night.
1. Children's stories. Australian.   [1. Night—
Fiction]   I. Peck, Beth, ill.   II. Title.
PZ7.ISBN 0-689-50363-6 W9593Ni 1985   [Fic]   85-7529

Published simultaneously in Canada by Collier Macmillan Canada, Inc.
Composition by Dix Type, Syracuse, New York
Printed by Connecticut Printers
Bound by Bookbinders, Inc.
Jersey City, New Jersey
First American Edition

Night
Outside

1

"Who's a clever boy?" asked James with his brown head bent over William's cage. It was a silly question but the first William had ever learned to answer, and you had to start with something easy if you wanted him to talk.

He answered at once in his croaking voice, "William's a clever boy." He turned his yellow head with a comical puppet's twist and fixed one black eye on James. James grinned and fingered the door of the budgerigar's cage.

"Don't take him out," said Anne quickly. "You know Dad doesn't like him flapping about the room." She glanced through the open kitchen door to the closed door of the bedroom where Dad was

3

lying in bed with the flu. Another groan and a bad-tempered mutter: he was getting crankier all the time. He was always cranky when he was sick, and Mum *would* have to be late home from work.

James sighed and dropped his hand to the table. He'd already had to put his bulldozer away because it was too noisy.

"Stop rocking the table," grumbled Anne. She was doing her homework. In theory it was not homework but a project, but anyway it was work that had to be done at home. She was making a neat drawing of wheat, copying from a colored photograph in the *Family Book of Knowledge*. Her colored pencils were pale and unsatisfying beside the rich colors of the photograph, but she worked on carefully, keeping an eye on James and the budgie while she listened for a groan or a curse from the bedroom. She had taken her father a cup of tea two hours ago and offered to switch his light on fifteen minutes ago, and she didn't know what else to do. She wished Mum would come home. It was time to switch the kitchen light on now, though the apartment was high up, on the sixth floor, and the kitchen window looked west over Seccombe Street.

James was fretful too. "I wish Mum'd come home. I'm getting hungry again."

"Too bad," snapped Anne. She was tired of being the elder—worrying about Dad and dinner when all James could worry about was being hungry; having to do this project while James played with William,

just because she happened to be a couple of years older. Maybe it was true, as Mum often said, that James's turn would come. But it seemed to Anne to be a long time coming. She piled her books together and went to switch on the light. This was an evening when she had better have the table set.

"Shift that cage, can't you, James? How can I put the cloth on?"

"Over his head," said James. "Go on, he'll think it's a snowstorm." But he lifted the cage off the table and hung it back on its stand in the corner. "What's your name?" he coaxed William.

William answered obligingly: "William Burt, Apartment 12, 23 Seccombe Street." James beamed at him.

Suddenly all three of them were still and listening. A tiny sound from the living room—Mum's key in the lock—at last! Both the children ran to the kitchen door.

"Sorry, loves," called Mum. "There in a second." She hurried into the bedroom to soothe her flu-stricken husband. First things first.

James wandered back to the budgie's cage. Anne seized a handful of knives and forks. She wished Mum luck, but the mutter of thunder from the bed-room didn't sound good.

Mum came in frowning and vexed, buttoning the smock she had changed into, and went at once to the stove.

"I'm starving," said James accusingly.

"Too bad," said Mum, just as Anne had. "Why didn't you cut a slice of bread?" But it wasn't a real question. She only asked it because she was upset.

"I've peeled the potatoes," said Anne. "I gave him a cup of tea. I didn't know what else . . . "

Mrs. Burt gave her a quick smile. "It's all right, love. Men are always cross when they're sick. They're no good at it."

"Was it the bus again?"

"Mostly. There was half an hour's overtime too; not worth ringing up if it hadn't been for the bus . . . Get those chops out, will you? . . . Overtime helps when you're saving for something like a house, and with your father sick—well, he ought to be glad, that's all."

Anne looked worried. "But he isn't *very* sick, is he? I mean it's only this week, and he'll get sick pay, won't he?"

"Of course he will. Only you're never quite sure how long it's going to take, and he used up some sick pay in May, and when you've got a plan and everything keeps going up . . . That's why he's so cranky, of course. He worries."

"I wish—" began Anne; and then she stopped quickly but it was too late. Mrs. Burt was upset and worried too. She banged the pan down hard on the stove.

"I know, I know, you wish I didn't have to work! As if I was saving up for a mink coat instead of a decent house for you kids, with a garden where you can

7

bring your friends! Do you think I like rushing off to one job and rushing home to another day after day? What between you and your father—"

"That's right, blame me and the kids."

It was Dad's furious voice from the kitchen door. He was standing there in his old flannel dressing-gown, his face drawn into lines and dark with stubble. And suddenly, ordinary crankiness and worry seemed to have swollen into something big and dark that filled the kitchen. James shrank quietly into the corner by William's cage. Anne crept over beside the refrigerator. Mrs. Burt jerked at the pan on the stove.

"Go back to bed, for goodness sake, unless you want pneumonia."

Mr. Burt laughed in a sneering, bitter way. "Go back to bed. With you shouting and throwing pots about. A man might as well try and rest in the zoo." He crossed to the kitchen sink. "A man's got a throat like sandpaper, wants a drop of water, the only way to get it in this place is to get it for himself." He drew a glass of water, took a sip, and dashed the rest into the sink. He rounded suddenly, glaring from red eyes. "Can I help it if I've got the flu?"

Mrs. Burt's eyes flamed back. "Who said you could? Can I help it if the buses are late?"

He roared. *"There's a thing called the telephone!"*

Mrs. Burt yelled. *"And they don't have them in buses!"*

Beside the refrigerator Anne was as cold and stiff as a stone. James in his corner was not so lucky; nervously fingering the door of William's cage he found himself with the budgie in his hand. His father lunged, gripping the table as he went.

"I've told you! You'll take notice of me, boy! I won't have that bird loose, making messes to be cleaned up! You'll do as you're told"—his hand closed on William and swung—"or no bird!" William was gone, flung through the open window six storeys above the street.

Anne felt herself shaking. James was rigid, staring at his father and slowly turning crimson. Then he unfroze.

"You might have broken his legs!" yelled James, and ran out of the room.

Anne heard him open the outer door and rush into the hall. The next moment, without knowing how, she found herself going after him: out in the hall, running, running, either to catch James or to get away from the apartment before some worse thing happened.

There was no time for the elevator. James's feet were pounding away down the concrete stairs, and Anne's pounded after him. She thought she heard her mother's voice call down the stairwell but she didn't look up. She was racing across the entrance hall of the house, out into Seccombe Street in the half-dark. There was James, crouched on the pavement under their kitchen window, searching for William. She ran to him, shouting. "James!"

And suddenly it was gone, the big dark thing that

had filled the kitchen and followed them down the stairs. It had blown away like smoke and vanished into something even bigger, a sort of peace or a sort of waiting. There were the streetlights, one beyond another, reaching away down the street into quietness, each one lonelier than the last and all of them waiting for dark. There was the high lift of the sky between buildings, a greenish glow beyond the lights. There was darkness creeping around corners and lying under walls. Anne stopped running and went forward into quietness, like the dark. She stooped over James.

"Don't be mad," she said. "Nothing's broken and he's not down here. He'll have flown."

James stood up. On the black pavement at his feet someone had written a word in white chalk. It was round and firm and clear, every letter perfect, and its whiteness seemed to shine in the evening light, a beautiful word.

ETERNITY.

2

Anne stared at the word on the pavement. She had seen it before, of course. Now that she thought about it, she had even seen it at some time written on a pavement in this round and flowing perfection. But never before had it seemed to flow outward in a great quiet ripple to meet the night.

"Look," she said to James.

"Eh? Yes, I know." He moved his feet and trod on the word. "If William was hurt he mightn't have flown. But he's not down here anyway. We'll have to find him."

"Yes," said Anne gladly. She knew she could not go back into that angry little apartment up there, not until the spreading quiet had had time to reach it.

"He must be scared, too," said James. "Where would he fly?"

Anne thought. "Back into another window?" At once she wished she hadn't thought of that, but then William did have to be found. It was confusing.

They stared up the cliffside of the building in which they lived, its red brick darkening in the night. A lot of windows in this wall were alight, but only three were open: one on the fourth floor, their own kitchen window, and one in the flat next to theirs.

"Mrs. Warburton," said James, looking at that one. "And the old bloke downstairs with the cat. We'll have to go back in." He sounded as though he didn't want to any more than she did.

"Well . . . ' said Anne. "The old bloke first, then. In case they hear us at Mrs. Warburton's and . . . "

"They can say what they like," said James roundly. "I'm not going in till we've found William. They can help it and he can't."

"Well, I know *that*. I'm not going in either. Only I don't think they *can* help it really. It's this house idea, and the money. They get worried and worked up. But it's for us."

"They needn't bother, then. We've always had the apartment and it's all right."

"A garden would be somewhere to go. Like now."

James was unforgiving. "If they didn't get worked up we wouldn't need somewhere to go." He went quietly to the doorway and listened. "It's all right. We"ll have to take the elevator. It's quieter, and

13

we've got to be quiet. Because I don't think William's flown back in, so we'll have to come out again."

"But if he's not in there, why do we have to go in?"

"He might be. I don't know, do I?"

Reluctantly, Anne crept after him into the building and across to the elevator.

The building was quiet, but its quietness was different from that of the night outside. All the closed doors seemed to listen. It was as well that the old man with the cat lived down on the fourth floor; he was rather deaf, and it took a long time to explain what they wanted. Then he was helpful and searched his flat carefully, letting James show him likely places in the folds of the curtains or shadows in corners. There was no sign of William. They had to take the elevator up to their own floor.

They saw at once that the door of their apartment was still open, as they had left it when they raced out. They would have to creep past that, down the hall and round a corner to Mrs. Warburton's door. From their kitchen, out through the open door, came a smell of burned chops and the sound of Dad's voice. It was still angry and desperate, not like the Dad they knew, and it sent Anne scurrying after James even while she listened.

"—not babies!" Dad was saying. "They'll come in when they're hungry!" Then the voice dropped to a worried note and said something about". . . need a breathing space . . . "

All right, thought Anne, if that was what he needed he could have it. She needed it too; she felt tight again all over. She was aching from being the elder—from school projects and house projects and listening doors and worried mums and dads. She was going back to the night outside, even if William was in Mrs. Warburton's apartment.

They had no trouble at all with Mrs. Warburton. Answering their ring, she took them quietly inside, heard their request, sat down and left them to search, all without a word. They crept about the flat, searching and whispering, failing to find a sign of William. Only when they were thanking her did Mrs. Warburton speak, and then quite softly.

"Dad drunk, is he, then?" said Mrs. Warburton.

Anne turned red. Listening doors! "He's got flu, that's all, and he's no good at it."

"Nasty old bag," she hissed as the door closed softly and safely behind them. James looked surprised and frowned her into silence. They crept back to the elevator and in two minutes were back outside.

There it was again, the wide quiet night. It was dark now. One car came down Seccombe Street and turned off. The lights stretched away into loneliness. Under the kitchen window the pavement spoke its beautiful word: ETERNITY. The aching tightness went away like a broken rubber band.

"I wonder where he'd fly to?" said James, frowning.

"The park," said Anne.

15

"That's a long way. How would he know?"

"*I* don't know, then. Only he hasn't flown back in and the park has the first trees."

They followed the lights down Seccombe Street toward the park.

"I'm starving," said James.

"Go home, then. You're supposed to go home when you're hungry."

"I'm not going home till I find William. Even if I starve to death."

Anne laughed suddenly. "Oh, Jimpy," she said, using the baby name that she hadn't even wanted to use for over a year.

"It's not funny," said James sternly.

"I know that. Only thinking of you starving to death under a tree in the park. Like being lost in the bush." She gave him a poke in the ribs. "I reckon you'll last the night. You're plump enough."

"I'm still starving."

They turned into the park, a wide darkness that held back the streets with their rows of square buildings, a darkness splashed with pools of yellow light. At first Anne wanted to stride deep into it. Then she wanted to stay close to James. The park was a breathing space, but not the sort that Dad had meant. It was a space that breathed.

Shrubs breathed quietly at her shoulder and trees breathed overhead. The pools of yellow light moved stealthily as the shadows of leaves shifted and stirred. And in the darkness, she could feel, there were people breathing too. It made the park a secret and dangerous place, a place where someone really might die of starvation under a tree.

She wondered who they were, these people who giggled softly behind bushes, who sat primly on lighted benches or were draped as dark shadows on the grass. What had they come here for? Not for coolness; it was not yet summer. She and James were both wearing sweaters though they had never meant to come running away from their kitchen. Had these people no kitchens of their own? No well-lit narrow spaces between walls? No living rooms with television sets? Why had they chosen this wide dark with its pale splashes of light and its breathing trees?

She tugged at James to draw him back to the street. They would never find William in this leafy, haunted, light-and-dark place. But James had reached his own conclusions about the park.

"It's too big," he said. "William's used to his cage, with just a room for outside. He wouldn't come here."

"If he did," said Anne, "he'll have to wait till morning. We'll never find him now."

"I'll just give him a call in case, now we're here." He moved into the shifting light under a lamp. "William! Come on, boy! Who's a clever boy? William!"

Anne felt hidden eyes turning toward them. "James!" she hissed. "People are listening."

"So what? They might know where he is." He walked back a little way toward the street and called again. But Anne stood still for a moment and her heart lifted.

There it was again, shining on the path at the edge of the light: ETERNITY, round and firm and perfect. It was here too, spreading its ripple of strangeness and quiet through the night.

Now she knew the people in the shadows. At least —no, she didn't, and she and James were going back to the street. But still she knew that among these people there might be spirits for whom a kitchen was simply too narrow and too bright.

"William!" shouted James. "Clever old boy— come on, William!" Someone giggled, but it didn't matter. Anne stepped over Eternity and went after James to the edge of the park. On the wide steps with the big stone columns at each side he stopped to call again, and this time there was an answer.

"Lost someone, have you, dears?"

A woman came out of the darkness behind them, out of the breathing park. A woman for whom the ordinary kitchen would have been too narrow and too bright.

3

To Anne, the woman seemed exactly the right sort of person to come out of the darkness and the park. She brought with her a new sort of seeing, so that everything looked clearer and yet stranger. Anne saw that this was not an ordinary night, upset by the disaster of William's being thrown away. It was a special, different, once-only night; a night that could call up disaster and then, when you ran away, tip you down a slippery-dip into strangeness. These were not the streets and park they knew, simply disguised by the night and the lights. The streets and park had been tipped into strangeness too; they were in some other part of some other world. The woman belonged to that world.

She was not old but nearly old. She wore a dark, shabby coat, and, draped over its shoulders, a very big silk scarf that the lights pricked into a pattern of purple and green and orange. Another big scarf was tied over her head like a hood, and it seemed to be patterned in red and blue and black. Gray wisps of hair from under the scarf blew around her face, which was thin and deeply wrinkled. She clutched a crumpled old handbag, and a big shopping bag hung from each arm. A queer smell hung about her; it reminded Anne of shabby butcher shops and stale refrigerators. She looked at the children with kind, faded eyes, but not as if she wanted to know about them. It was more like someone in a shop waiting to hear what you wanted to buy.

"Lost someone, have you, dears?" she said.

James told her at once, as he would have told the person in the shop. "William, our budgie. Yellow and blue, with stripes on his neck. He—got dropped out of the window. It's a high window. He'd probably fly."

The woman thought about it. "A budgie. Didn't ought to drop him out the window, you know. But he wouldn't fly far. Where do you live?"

Anne told her. "Apartment 12, 23 Seccombe Street. It's not far."

"Red brick block with the glass door and the old houses behind," said the woman. James looked astonished that she should know it at once, but Anne only laughed inside. Of course the woman would know. "He didn't fly back in?" They shook their heads. "He'll be nearer home than this. Better find him before some of my cats do." She seemed to be thinking, and they waited. "Come with Ruby, dears," she said at last. "I'm nearly done here."

She set off at a slow side-to-side sort of walk, not down Seccombe Street but across it. The big bright scarves went flapping away into darkness and the children ran after them: James because he was sure she would know about William, and Anne because this once-only night had to be taken as it came. The scarves plunged into the blackness of a lane, and the children stumbled in behind them. Anne wondered what strangeness the night had to show in this lane. At other times it was a dreary, empty place running between the backs of shops. There were blank walls and a few dim little windows; doors and gates kept locked unless goods were being delivered; stacks of empty crates rising above the walls; and a blank wall suddenly cutting it off at the end. But tonight— what? There were tiny sounds in the air, and a sense of sly waiting.

The children groped their way, but the woman walked ahead as if she didn't need to see. Perhaps she had forgotten them, for when James spoke she stopped and turned her head in a startled way. "Eh?" she said.

"Have you got a lot of cats?" asked James again, remembering what she had said before.

The woman peered at him. "Near a hundred, coming and going," she said at last. "Sometimes more, sometimes less."

"A hundred cats!" James was agog.

"Shush, now," said the woman, "and stay back. You'll scare the poor things. They don't know you, see. They don't know nobody, only old Ruby."

She went on toward the end wall, and the children waited. By now their eyes were so used to the dark that they could see her against the whitewashed wall. She gave a soft crooning call—and around her the darkness was suddenly alive and moving. Shadows flowed down from walls and along gutters, shadows twined about Ruby's feet. There were deep, dangerous growls, fierce spittings, murmuring cries. These were not tame housecats but jungle cats.

"Wow!" whispered James. Full of delight, Anne hushed him.

Ruby was stooping, taking something from the shopping bags and putting it down here and there. The sharp, unpleasant smell, of butchershops and stale refrigerators, grew strong. Cats growled and spat, dragging away from each other what Ruby had given them. She crooned to them and watched.

After a minute she came back, stopping in a surprised way when she saw the children and bending to peer into their faces. They saw that her own face was softened and content, as though she herself had been hungry and was fed.

"A budgie, wasn't it?" she said. "Find him before the cats do. Nearer home. Scared, poor mite."

They went back down the lane.

James asked, "Why do you feed the cats?"

"Eh?" said Ruby. "Poor things. Who else is there?"

"It must take a lot of stuff," said Anne. "Where do you get it all?" It wasn't a real question, for she felt sure she would never know the answer. She asked so that Ruby would go on remembering that she and James were there. She must not let Ruby lose them. On this strange, once-only night in this other world, Ruby was the only guide they had.

Ruby gave the sort of answer Anne expected. "Eh? Here and there. It's wonderful what you can get if you know where. And there's help. Mrs. Haitch, now. A good woman, her."

Anne was going to ask about Mrs. Haitch, but at the entrance to the lane, where it now seemed light after the darkness inside, she saw something that made her forget that question. It was there again, written this time on the wall, as shining and flowing as ever: ETERNITY.

"Who writes that?" said Anne quickly.

"Eh?" said Ruby. She peered at the writing and moved back suddenly. "He's around all right, then. I thought so." She seemed awed, looking at the word from a respectful distance.

"Who is it?" cried Anne, for all the magic of the night was in that word and she needed an answer.

"That's Cyril, that is," said Ruby slowly. "He's a

scholar, that one. There's not many gets to the bottom of him."

Anne was sure of it, but she needed to know more. She planted herself firmly between Ruby and the street, gazed at the quiet shining word on the wall, and waited.

"Eternity, that is," Ruby explained. "He puts it about so people won't forget. Don't show up often, how could he? He's got too much ground to cover."

He would have: all the worlds and the spaces between.

"What does it mean?" asked Anne.

"Eh? Well, dear—it's Eternity, isn't it? Out past here. Where things get fed." With a weaving, side-to-side motion she flowed around Anne and out into Seccombe Street. James went confidently beside her, and Anne followed wondering.

The lonely lights led them down Seccombe Street.

"I'm starving," said James.

"Eh?" Ruby peered at him. She seemed upset.

"We've had no dinner at all," James boasted, "and it was hours ago."

"Better get home, then. Your mum'll be after you."

"They'll still be fighting," said James. "Anyway, I'm not going home till we find William."

"Shut up, James," said Anne. Ruby was looking confused and worried, the wrinkles on her face all running down. And the night had already shown that its strangeness wasn't always safe or pretty. What sort of revenge might it take on fighting parents? "It wasn't hours ago," she told Ruby, "only about half an hour. And they don't want us home yet, they want a breathing space. They said so."

Ruby weaved on in silence. After a minute she said, "It's them should be out here, then. An apartment's no breathing space."

"They couldn't," said Anne quickly. "Dad's got flu. That's why he's cranky, he's no good at it . . . That and the apartment, like you said. They want a house and garden. So they both have to work. They get tired . . ."

"Ah," said Ruby. "Eternity." If that was some kind of charm, Anne hoped it was the right kind.

"Have you got an apartment?" she asked daringly.

"Not me, dear. I've got my little place. I mostly keep dry. Couldn't afford an apartment, any road. Too many mouths to feed."

"I can see our kitchen window!" cried James.

There it was, the dark bulk of the building ahead hung with lighted windows, and the one light that came from the Burts' kitchen. It was like a lighthouse, partly a warning to keep off and partly a promise of safety beyond the sea.

Ruby paused under a streetlight, all the brilliance of her scarves lit up and moving gently in the breeze. Anne suddenly hoped that the breeze would not strengthen into a wind, lifting and spreading those bright scarves into sails and carrying Ruby up beyond the lights. Her face had turned dreamy; she made soft

27

chirruping sounds. "Where's the poor boy, then?" she crooned, and veered aside to lift the lid of a mailbox and peer inside.

They went slowly on toward their building, crossing the street from side to side. Ruby searched doorways and front-door shrubs, mailboxes, the telephone booth, streetlight brackets and all shadowy corners, chirruping and crooning as she went.

"William!" called James from the entrance to a parking lot. "Clever boy, William! Here, boy."

Anne searched too, for William had to be found; but she knew that if they found him now the night would not let them go. Not yet. It had more than this up its sleeve.

They reached their own building and Anne showed Ruby where Eternity lay on the sidewalk. Ruby walked carefully around it muttering, "Ah, he's a deep one," and examined the corners of window frames.

They searched carefully the faces of the building that lay along Seccombe Street and along Collins Street running down the side, for Ruby was sure that William would not have flown far from here. The next building in Seccombe Street was joined to theirs by a high brick wall; but from Collins Street a narrow paving ran along the back of the building, where the garbage cans were put out and collected.

"He's likely in there, poor mite," said Ruby.

It was nearly as dark as the lane had been, with only a little light from one or two lighted windows above. A high brick wall cut the paving off from the empty cottages behind. It was mainly because she knew they were there that Anne could pick out a row of garbage cans lining the farther end of the paving.

Ruby went forward with her air of not needing to see. Anne followed—and stopped so sharply that James bumped into her from behind. The farthest garbage can was suddenly lit up, a yellow plastic beacon lit from inside. For one moment its black lid gaped toward them; a shadow-show of humped shapes and an old shoe appeared on its side; then it was gone, and the can beside it glowed suddenly green.

One by one, along the row toward them, each can flared and blinked: violet, orange, green, yellow. The children stared, transfixed, but Ruby called out softly:

"Reg? It's Ruby, dear."

4

Something came softly to meet Ruby: the shadow, whatever it was, that had lit the cans to beacons. Straining her eyes, Anne saw that it was a man, thin and straight, carrying something in each hand.

"How's business, dear?" said Ruby.

"Bad," said the man, and came further into the light. He wore a neat gray overcoat and carried a suitcase in one hand and a big flashlight in the other. "Nothing in this lot," he said, and glanced sharply at the children. "What have you got there, Rube?"

Ruby's voice was uncertain and a little troubled. "They lost a budgie. They live in here. Got sent out while their mum and dad have a fight."

The man looked up at lighted windows and shook his head. "Marvellous, ain't it?"

"The girl's a deep one," said Ruby, astonishing Anne. Was she really a deep one? Like Cyril who hung Eternity on walls and laid it on pavements so that people wouldn't forget? "Call your bird, dear," said Ruby to James. "He's likely waiting for you in there."

James went further along the paving and called softly. In a little while he was back. "He's not there. I'm *starving.*"

Ruby gave him a brooding look and rummaged in one of her bags. She gave up and closed the bag jealously. "You wouldn't have something they could eat, I s'pose?" she asked Reg.

"Not me. Don't see that sort of stuff these days. They can't afford it." He moved the suitcase, making it tinkle. "Only one or two bits Mrs. Haitch might be interested in."

"We better get on, then," said Ruby, "or we'll be taken for burgulars."

Anne glanced up, half expecting to see the "burgulars" walking up the wall on their fly feet, inserting cunning hosepipes into windows and sucking out the things they wanted. But the wall was bare. They went out of the narrow darkness into Collins Street.

"No knowing where your budgie's got to," said Ruby. "Eternity, maybe."

"No," said James firmly.

Reg had slipped across the street to where two or

three garbage cans waited outside gates. Ruby stood under a light, her face wrinkled with thought. Her draperies moved slyly, a rippling of purple and green and red. Across the street the garbage cans lit up in turn, orange and violet and yellow. The yellow one stayed alight a moment longer; the shadow of Reg's hand moved in it before the light went out.

"What's he *doing?*" said James.

"Shush," said Anne. She wanted to ask too, but Ruby was working something out. Reg came slipping back across the street, fastening his suitcase as he came. Ruby watched; only when he stood with them again on the pavement did she speak.

"There's these old houses, then. Your bird might be there. I gotta go there any road." She looked at Reg and waited for a moment, but he didn't speak. "You been round there?" she asked him. "Anyone about?"

"I don't go regular," said Reg, "but I might look in tonight. People throw stuff over . . . He's around all right, but I'd say he's out working."

The two turned together toward the first shabby gate. Anne and James looked at each other, then silently followed.

The old cottages stood side by side, hopelessly waiting to be pulled down and turned into more apartments. The gate of the first sagged open, but its single front window was broken and boarded up. The second had no gate at all; the glass of its window gleamed at them blackly. Ruby squeezed through the first gate saying, "Quiet, dears. Don't scare the poor things."

"More cats, then," whispered James. "I hope William's all right."

"He wouldn't come down near cats," Anne whispered back.

They crept after Ruby and Reg through the small weedy garden, along a broken path that led around the house into darkness. They had to feel their way slowly; the two strange spirits who led them were lost in the dark ahead. Then they felt space opening up and heard the jungle-sounds of cats, and Reg stopped them with a hand and a word from the dark.

Ruby came back, breathing in a satisfied way, and Reg slipped off. His torch flashed once or twice in the yard, and there was a jingle of metal. Now again they could see dimly.

Ruby was peering into eaves and at window-frames, chirruping softly. "Call your bird, dears. . . . Chrrp, chrrp . . . He won't be inside, it's all boarded up."

James called and Anne searched. Reg came back and they all went on to the second house.

This time there were no cats, but a missing window gaped blackly. Ruby listened at it while Anne and James searched and Reg's flashlight made quick flashes in the yard.

"No one about," she said at last. "You can look inside."

"In *there?*" said Anne. She could never go through that black gape; not without Ruby. She felt the silken flutter of scarves as the woman stooped over her.

"Ruby wouldn't send you anywhere nasty, dear."

"I'll go," said James.

"Jimpy! You're not to!"

"Good man," said Reg from behind, and lifted James through the window. "Want a torch? Keep an eye open for anything useful." He passed his light through the window to James. Anne and Ruby leaned in at the window, waiting tensely.

The torch flashed once or twice, but light from the street came through the front window. "William!" called James. "Come on, William! Who's a clever boy?"

And whispering hoarsely out of the shadows came an answer: "William's a clever boy."

"He's here! He's here! William—what's your name, boy?"

"William Burt, Apartment 12, 23 Seccombe Street. William's a clever boy." There was a soft sound and a movement of air.

"I've got him. I've got him!" James was standing with cupped hands.

"There now," said Ruby.

"Who's that?" whispered Anne. For something had come through a door beyond James: a pale figure in the faint yellow light from the street. She felt Ruby stiffen.

"He's there, then," she whispered. "Hush, now, dear, don't frighten the poor thing. He don't know you, see. It's only Cyril."

"*Cyril!* Not—the Eternity man?"

"Him, dear. Hush, Ruby's here."

The white shape came closer. James saw it in the midst of his excitement. "I've found him!" he cried to it. And Cyril spoke.

His voice was gentle and wondering, so that Anne felt all her tightness relaxing. "It talks," said Cyril. "The little bird . . . I heard it."

Perhaps James too would have been startled now that his excitement had cooled, if the white figure of Cyril had not spoken so gently. But the streetlight showed a white head bending over James, and James showing him William.

"Do you want to hold him? He'll sort of sit on your hand. Come on, William."

He won't, thought Anne, he's shy of strangers . . . if he flies inside there I suppose James can get him again.

But it seemed that this time William was not shy. The bent heads straightened, and Cyril stepped back with the bird at rest in his hands. Now, as it happened, he was facing the other window: the one that held the dark shapes of Ruby and Anne with Reg behind them. He started, held his cupped hands to his chest, turned quickly and slipped away like a white ghost in the shadows.

"Hey!" called James indignantly, and Ruby called too.

"It's all right, Cyril, it's only old Ruby."

It was too late. A door creaked and closed. The Eternity man had gone, taking William with him.

5

"Hey!" yelled James again. He had run after the Eternity man. Through the door they could see his torch-beam strike down a hall.

"Jimpy, come back!" shouted Anne in a frenzy.

"Well now . . ." muttered Ruby, baffled, and behind her Reg laughed with a sort of glee.

"It's not funny!" yelled James, suddenly reappearing at the window and beginning to scramble through. "He's snitched William!" Still chuckling, Reg helped him down.

"Eh?" said Ruby with a silken rustle of scarves. "Not snitched him, dear, not Cyril. He's a gentle soul. Startled, that's all, and forgot all about you. He don't like to be caught by people, see."

Anne at least did see. Now that fright of his coming and going had faded, it seemed quite right. It was just how Cyril would come and go on this once-only night. Of course he wouldn't like to be caught by people, the man from all the worlds and the spaces between.

"But what are we going to *do?*" said James. "I'm not going home without William and that's that."

Ruby fluttered again. "Well, dear . . . I suppose we'll have to go after him."

"You won't find Cyril in a hurry," chuckled Reg, taking his flashlight back from James. "No knowing where he'll get to now."

"We can follow his trail, can't we?" Anne suggested. "Won't he go on putting Eternity about?"

"So he will, dear, soon as he's over his fright. And that'll be the minute he gets outside . . . The girl's a deep one," Ruby muttered to Reg. "But the boy's hungry."

"Sorry I can't help," said Reg. "Have to leave you. I've got my round to finish." He raised his flashlight in farewell and went off around the house, his suitcase chinking. Anne thought he didn't believe they would ever find Cyril or get William back.

"I don't like him much," she muttered. "He doesn't care."

"Never you mind Reg, dear," said Ruby.

"I don't mind him," James declared. "It's that other one. Aren't we going after him? Come on."

As they groped their way back through the weedy garden Anne secretly wondered if Reg might not be right. For hadn't Ruby stood with her bright silks stirring and said that William might be in Eternity? And hadn't he vanished with the Eternity man?

From the empty gateway they looked up and down Collins Street. It seemed bright after the darkness of the yard, but there was no one in sight.

"He won't go back to Seccombe Street," Anne guessed, "because he's been there already."

"Anyhow, he didn't come this way," added James. "He'd have had to go past you to get out here. There must be a back lane or something, out to the next street."

He and Anne turned toward the next street after Seccombe, and Ruby followed as if she were in two minds. The new street was a quiet one, dimly lit. A few curtained windows glowed from lines of terraced cottages. There were shadow-rows of garbage cans down each pavement. Far ahead one of them blinked into orange light and out again. James turned back to Ruby.

"That Reg has come this way, too. What's he *doing* with those bins?"

"Eh?" said Ruby, weaving on from side to side. "Well, dear. It's wicked the stuff people waste, you know, and other people without. Reg unwastes it . . . yes, that's what he does. There's fine things in fine houses, and people dusting 'em every day, that

Reg has unwasted. But mostly it's little things some-one might just happen to want only they never could have 'em without Reg. Wasted, see."

Anne asked a sly question. "Is that Eternity too? Where things get unwasted?"

"Eh? No use asking old Ruby about that, dear. Cyril's the one to ask. He's the scholar."

And here, sure enough, was the mouth of a dark lane. And there was the word, round and simple and beautiful: ETERNITY. It was as if the white figure that carried off William had laid a white word to guide them.

"That's it, that's it, he came this way!" James ran ahead, searching the pavement for the next sign.

"There now," said Ruby, but she still seemed hesitant.

"You don't think we'll find him, do you?" whispered Anne.

"I wouldn't say that, dear. It might take a while."

Ahead in the dark, another garbage can woke and blinked out. The breeze drew a whisper from Ruby's scarves and a sour breath from her shopping bags. Strange figures from a strange night: Reg and Ruby and the vanished white figure of the Eternity man. And still the night would not let Anne and James go.

James, watching the pavement, passed the next sign and never saw it. Anne found it hanging on a wall. Ruby looked at it in silence. James said, "I'm *starving*. I'm *really* starving now."

"Shut up, James. You don't think you're the only one, do you?"

"I never said I was, did I? I just said I'm starving."

Ruby took root on the pavement, all the lines on her face running down. "It can't go on, dears," she said.

"But how can it stop?" cried Anne. "I promise you it's only an hour past dinnertime. Nobody starves in an hour. And there's William. Don't take any notice of James."

"I'm not going home yet anyway," said James bravely.

"All right, then! Come on and shut up! You know it can't really go on forever, so why do you keep wasting it? Look—is that something white?" She hurried James on, hissing into his ear, while she sneaked a glance behind to make sure that Ruby followed. They must not lose Ruby—she must not lose them—it was not yet time.

James found the next Eternity, showing clear, under a light at a street corner. "What's he doing?" said James. "It's across the corner. You can't tell which way."

"Likely he's gone around there," said Ruby. She sounded more alert, as though this one word told more than the others had done. They turned the corner and Ruby went ahead. If they had been fishing Anne would have said that Ruby had a nibble. She hissed a second warning to James and followed.

Ruby passed another Eternity without pausing or

speaking and a little later crossed the street. She had not even looked for a sign; she crossed as though she saw the white shape of Cyril himself, and the children followed. Ruby led them to the next intersection and paused, and they all saw the sign again.

"There now!" said Ruby, her colored silks weaving. All her uncertainty seemed to have gone. "I should've thought. Mrs. Haitch."

"Mrs. Haitch!" cried Anne, for this mysterious name had been spoken before. "Who's Mrs. Haitch?"

"Eh?" said Ruby. "A friend of Cyril's, dear. A good woman. I never knew her turn her back on anything hungry." She glanced broodingly at James.

"She must be a friend of yours too," said Anne.

"A friend of everyone, Mrs. Haitch. But Cyril's not got many friends, there's not many understands him. I should've seen he'd go to Mrs. Haitch." She turned confidently into the next street, her scarves aflutter.

It was a narrow old street; its terraces of tiny cottages seemed to whisper to each other across it, for their front doors rose straight from the pavement. The first was in fact an old corner store, with a window glowing above, where the storekeeper lived. Here and there, other small shops were embedded in the rows of cottages: dark windows with names painted on their glass.

"Thomas & Son, Butchers," read James; and a little later, "Family Chemist." More cottages, and a window with shoes in a row. A pair of very dark windows painted with flowers. MARY HUNTER, ANTIQUES, said one; and the other, SECONDHAND GOODS. Between them stood a white door with an iron knocker and a slit for letters.

Ruby seized the knocker and beat on the door.

6

"Mary Hunter," read James. "Is *she* Mrs. Haitch?"

Ruby didn't answer but knocked again. Footsteps shuffled, a chain clattered, the door opened a crack, and a woman's voice said, "Oh. Ruby." The door closed again.

It opened wider: a sense of crowding darkness, beyond it a strip of mustard light, and outlined against the light a short, round figure that must surely be Mrs. Haitch herself. "Come in, love," she said. "Who's that you've got?"

Ruby edged into the crowding dark while the children hesitated in the doorway. They could hear Ruby explaining them to Mrs. Haitch. "They got sent out while their mum and dad had a fight. The boy's hungry. Cyril's got their budgie. Is he here?"

"Oh," said Mrs. Haitch. "It's *their* budgie, is it?" Her voice was flat, as though she were not pleased. Anne felt somehow guilty and hung back till a plump arm came forth and drew her inside. "Go through, then," said Mrs. Haitch. "Can you find your way?"

It was not easy. There seemed to be only a narrow strip of floor, no more than a foot wide, between dark, looming shapes with corners. Ruby went surely after Mrs. Haitch toward the glowing mustard curtain; Anne and James stumbled over things that rattled and were tripped by sly wooden feet. Something soft and feathery fondled Anne's neck and she almost screamed. They reached the curtain and Mrs. Haitch held it aside. They all squeezed past into a tiny space between stacked shelves. A small electric bulb on a long cord washed yellow light over the goods on the shelves and over Mrs. Haitch herself. The one was as strange as the other.

The shelves were packed with mottled mirrors, bits of old iron, broken vases, empty frames, china people with heads or arms broken off, bottles without tops and tops without bottles; an enormous hoard of things too many to be seen. Mrs. Haitch was short and plump, with a face as soft and smooth as a flower and with rich-red hair in heavy waves. Her eyes were brown and sharp, but when they were not looking at you they were soft. She wore tiny earrings that suddenly flashed with fire, a tight red dress and over it a wonderful shawl embroidered with faded flowers. The shawl had a very deep silk fringe and swept down to the tops of her blue felt slippers. It was pinned in front with a brooch of green glass.

Mrs. Haitch let the curtain drop, turned to one corner of the shelves and vanished. Ruby vanished too. Anne and James found that in this corner the shelves did not meet. They too slipped through the gap, into a room.

It took some time to see the room properly. This was partly because it was a big room with a high ceiling and partly because it was lit by another small electric bulb that hung on a twisted flex from the dimness above. At first it seemed like a dining room, for there was a large old table with three knobbly-backed chairs. But it was also a living room; a shabby easy chair stood near the table, and two old armchairs in one corner had their high backs turned to the room. At last they saw that it was most of all a kitchen.

There was an old gas stove, squat and bandy-legged; a sink that was partly white enamel and partly black iron; a counter with a brown china teapot, an electric kettle and a toaster; an old green refrigerator; kitchen cupboards under the counter, and above it long shelves that held china and canisters. Even these were different from those in an ordinary kitchen. No two plates or cups were of the same size or pattern, but all of them were richly colored, like a garden full of different flowers. The canisters were even odder:

colored glass, patterned china, carved wood, dull metal with a coppery glint; birds of paradise, pansies and roses, twining branches, animal faces.

Mrs. Haitch was already at the kitchen counter, her shawl thrown back from her shoulders, busy with the toaster and a loaf of bread. Ruby sat on the edge of one of the chairs and watched the slicing of bread. The only other person in the room seemed to be Reg. He sat in the easychair near the table, and on the table lay his suitcase. It was open, so that at last James and Anne could see what it held: folded newspapers, two halves of a red-and-gold plate, a flower-shaped spoon with its silver worn off, two large rusted hinges, a file without a handle.

Reg did not seem surprised to see Ruby and the children. "You tracked him, then," he said with a chuckle, reached for the spoon in his suitcase and began to straighten its handle.

Anne, too, perched on the edge of a chair, her eyes taking in everything. Here the strangeness and wonder of the night were thickest, like sugar at the bottom of a cup. It was in the silently crowding dark of the shop where there was no room for people; in that secret place where shelves were packed with waste or unwasting; in the kitchen that was like no other kitchen; in the sharp, soft eyes of Mrs. Haitch and the rich-and-poor things she wore. From one shelf a clockface looked down between the heads of two snarling lions. It said half-past eight, if such things could be believed.

James did not sit down. He stood by Reg and looked around the room, frowning. "Tracked who?" he challenged.

Reg only chuckled again, putting the spoon back in his suitcase. From the corner, from behind the tall back of an armchair, came a well-known croaking whisper.

"I'm a wicked chap," said William.

James stiffened and swung that way.

"Hush, dear," murmured Ruby without looking away from the bread.

"James—don't—" said Anne, getting up quickly.

Mrs. Haitch filled the kettle and switched it on.

James hesitated, looking obstinate, then strode to the corner with Anne following. There was an old electric radiator, a round rusty dish on legs with an element shaped like a pinecone glowing in the center. The two armchairs were drawn up to it, and in one of them sat Cyril, small and white in ragged white overalls with his white head bent. William was perched on one finger, looking chirpy and pecking at a crust that Cyril held in his other hand.

Cyril looked up with far, blue eyes, and down again. Anne thought he hadn't seen them; his face was very quiet. She found herself smiling and sat down in the other armchair to watch.

"You've got our budgie," said James, still challenging but not too loudly.

Cyril crooned softly. "The little bird . . ."

William cocked a friendly eye at James and hopped

on Cyril's finger. "Where's the cat? Where's the cat? Where's the cat?" he said rapidly. "William Burt, Apartment 12, 23 Seccombe Street. I'm a wicked chap, a wicked chap." He pecked at the crust again.

James was indignant but baffled. William was a mean and lazy talker and generally shy with strangers. He put out a hand invitingly, but William didn't come. After a moment James let his hand drop. He wanted to put it out again, to take William away from Cyril; but he couldn't. He could only say again, "You've got our budgie."

Cyril looked up for a moment and spoke. His voice seemed to come from as far away as his eyes. "Nobody's bird, this one," he explained. "His own bird, this one."

James whirled and strode away.

"Sit down, then," said Mrs. Haitch, "while the toast's hot. Syrup?" She pushed a chair into place for James and poured a cup of tea, then drew a second chair out for Anne. The room was full of warmth and the smell of hot toast. Anne sniffed hungrily—but then she found Cyril's far blue eyes resting on her, watching her. The scholar, the Eternity man, the one who could tell her about this once-only night—he was looking at her.

She leaned forward and put her finger lightly on William's back. "He's nice, isn't he?" she said.

Cyril smiled, shy and gentle. "He talks."

"You write Eternity, don't you?" said Anne,

stroking William. "I've seen it, it's . . . beautiful. What does it mean?"

Cyril's eyes had gone away again. He said nothing, but crooned to William. Anne waited for a moment. She was about to stand up, disappointed, when at last he spoke.

"Eternity . . ." said Cyril.

She waited again. He leaned forward, white hair framing his white face, and whispered very secretly, "It's here. It's now."

He sat back, watching Anne to see if she had understood. She nodded, for she had suspected it all along. That was what the mischievous night had done when she and James and William came into it: it had caught all three of them and tipped them down a slippery-dip into strangeness, a different world, Eternity.

"William's a clever boy. Where's the cat? Where's the cat?"

Cyril leaned forward again, eager and secretive. "And what will it be tomorrow?" he whispered. "Eh? When you wake up in your bed, what will it be?"

She stared. She had thought that the night would let them go and tomorrow they would be in their own world.

"Eternity!" whispered Cyril, full of triumph. "It'll be Eternity!" He shook with silent laughter.

"But what *is* it?" cried Anne.

Cyril offered the crust to William, crooning. She

thought he would tell her no more, but suddenly he leaned forward again.

"It's the end of the world," he said softly, watching her. She nodded again, for she could believe it even if she didn't understand. "And where's the end of the world?" he asked slyly.

"Here?" guessed Anne. There was surely no stranger place.

"Ah . . . and where will it be when you get home, eh?"

"Still here?"

Cyril shone with triumph. "There! It'll be there! Wherever you are, that's the end of the world. Whenever it is, that's Eternity. You think about that. It's a mystery, that is. It's The Mystery."

7

It was too much of a mystery for Anne. She could only stare at Cyril. Mrs. Haitch spoke from the kitchen table.

"That's ‚enough, Cyril. Don't puzzle the child, she's had no dinner. Come and eat your toast, love, and never mind him."

"She's deep," explained Ruby. She was sitting with her colored silks at rest and the lines on her face softened, watching James eat. "She won't mind."

Anne went to the table. Something had been between her fingers and had slipped away. China and canisters, bright with birds and flowers that had never been, shone softly down from their shelves in the faded yellow light. Mrs. Haitch in her flowing shawl fingered the broken plate in Reg's suitcase.

"Pretty, that. Not worth much mended. Fifty cents the lot, Reg, .if you like."

"Now that's not like you, Mrs. Haitch. There's four pieces there. Make it a dollar."

Mrs. Haitch laughed sharply. "I'm not a charity, you know. What about cleaning and repairs? What about the stock I've got to keep and the time I've got to keep it? Seventy-five."

"Done," said Reg energetically, unloading his case on to the table. It seemed he could hardly wait to get back to the night outside and go on with his work of unwasting. Mrs. Haitch fixed her brown eyes sharply on James.

"And how did your budgie get out?" she asked.

James, full of toast, began to tell her in detail. Anne listened without hearing and watched in a dream. The Eternity man was hidden again behind the high back of the armchair; but Anne felt other eyes looking into her, and when she searched for them she found they were the dark eyes of Mrs. Haitch. Little sparks of fire winked sharply from her earrings.

"It'll be all right, love," said Mrs. Haitch. "You come and help me find Reg's money."

Anne stood up, dreamily obedient, and followed Mrs. Haitch from the room. In the little space between the shelves she stopped to fumble for a light switch.

"Fights don't last," she said. "Looking for Eternity, that's all they are. Your folk are out in the street by now, looking for you instead."

"They couldn't," said Anne. "Dad's got flu. That's what upset him."

"Flu or not. You take it from me. They're looking for you, out of their minds with worry." She pressed the switch and drew back the curtain. "Just time to show you *my* Eternity."

The shop was now lit with the same faded light as the kitchen. It brought out of the dark a silent looming crowd of old furniture, tall and heavy and dark, seeming to press forward into the narrow space that was left. Carved panels shone, yellow mirrors winked, ironwork twisted and curled. Corners and pegs were draped and festooned with faded silk and velvet, strings of beads, ropes of feathers. Every flat surface was crowded with smaller things: boxes of wood or brass or silver, others covered in velvet or seashells; lamps with tall glass chimneys; glasses and plates and bottles and vases and trays; faded pictures and yellowed books. Somehow Mrs. Haitch managed to move in and out among it all, and from unnoticed showcases and hidden corners she brought out sudden, unexpected things.

A pendant of sapphire set in silver. "Pretty, that. A butterfly's wing, that blue is."

A green glass bowl with a silver lid on which perched a silver bee. "For honey. Nice, isn't it?"

A vase, amber against the light but a deep purple-

blue if you held it the other way. A necklace of small blue birds. A tiny clock hung with silver spiderwebs caught in enamel. A box on which carved dragons writhed, a smoky-gold candlestick, a crystal scent bottle.

"Pretty, that."

"Has all this been unwasted?"

Mrs. Haitch smiled. "Not by Reg, any road. Just old stuff that nobody wants these days, so I give it a home till somebody else does. *I* like it." She moved off again, and Anne heard the chink of money. "Everyone's got their own Eternity, love, and this is mine. All I've got, any road. Your mum's and dad's is making a good place for all of you to live. Let's hope they don't have to lose it and make do with an apartment."

Anne fingered the carved box, and the dragons gaped their jaws at her. "Ruby's Eternity is feeding things. Reg's . . ."

"Is making a business for himself."

"And Cyril's?"

"Cyril talks a lot of sense, I don't say he doesn't. But there's not much to it, really. Eternity's for ever and ever, isn't that right? So every minute's got to be in it: today and tomorrow and all the rest. Nothing in that."

If you looked at it like that . . . "But he said it was the end of the world."

From somewhere Mrs. Haitch brought out a green glass ball in a mesh of rope. "A float off a fishing net,

60

that is. The shape of the world, isn't it? Now where's the end of that?"

Anne looked and thought. The end of the ball is wherever you put your finger. The magic of the night was a wisp of smoke, twining and curling into new shapes . . . and Mrs. Haitch's dark eyes watched her steadily.

"Don't you go turning us all into fairies, love, or monsters, either. Me and Ruby and Reg and Cyril, we're maybe not like the people you know. But there's one thing you can see, isn't there?"

Anne shook her head. Mrs. Haitch smiled: an odd smile, as if she were hurt.

"Come on, now, love. *We're all old losers, making do.*"

"You're not, you're not! You do—different things! Things other people don't have room for—"

"There's Ruby, feeding stray cats because she's got no one of her own to feed. There's Reg making all the business he can out of trashcans. Me that loves rich things, making do with other people's cast-offs. Cyril—just looking. But you, you're young, with a good mum and dad. You've still got Eternity."

"There's another thing," said Anne in a muffled voice. "Besides what you said. *You're all brave.*" They were still her four strange spirits of the night, free and different, doing things that other people didn't have room for; Eternity people.

Mrs. Haitch smiled again and put a gentle hand on her shoulder. "Don't you worry about us, love.

There's another world for you—and your mum and dad looking for you, out of their minds with worry."

The magic was still twining this way and that in her mind, but now Anne knew what it meant. The once-only night was letting her go at last.

"We have to go home!" she said, suddenly anxious for her worried mum and dad.

"That's right, love," said Mrs. Haitch.

8

They went back between the shelves to the kitchen, Anne hurrying in front. The clock, looking out between lions' heads, said half-past nine.

"Come on, Jimpy, quick! We've got to go home."

James had finished all the toast. "I won't go without William," he said, but not quite certainly.

"Get him, then," said Anne, and stood waiting to see. On this night, and in Mrs. Haitch's place, only the needed thing would happen.

James marched across to the armchair in the corner. He stood there, looking baffled and angry. Cyril had tucked William into a pocket, which he held safe with one thin hand. Lost in his secret world he never saw James's accusing stare, so James turned it on Ruby.

She looked at him vacantly, for she had done all she could. The bird was found, James was fed, and Ruby had handed over to Mrs. Haitch.

James's eyes fell away from her and appealed instead to Reg.

"Seventy-five," said Reg, counting coins. "Thanks, Mrs. Haitch."

James did what all the others had done: he turned to Mrs. Haitch.

She had taken off her wonderful sweeping shawl and was putting on a patchy fur coat. "Best leave it to me," she said, answering him. "I've an old cage somewhere. Hurry, now, or they'll have the police after you."

"But will William be *all right?*"

"I'll see to it. Say good night, now."

James and Anne said one good night to the three odd spirits in the kitchen. They hardly seemed to hear. Reg nodded, briskly fastening his suitcase. Ruby smiled a little and continued to rest. The Eternity man was invisible. Mrs. Haitch led the children away through the shop.

It was cold outside. The lights were few and lonely. Mrs. Haitch, a round shape in the fur coat, took them quickly down the narrow street past closed doors and dark shop windows.

"Can we come back?" asked Anne. She really wondered: could they?

"You'll want to know about your bird," said Mrs.

Haitch; and that must surely mean they could. "Don't worry, now. He'll be all right."

James tracked their way by the white words on the pavements, but Anne watched streets and corners, looking ahead and now and then behind. The magic had let them go as she had known it would; the night was tipping them back into their own world. Yet it had shown them a door that they could find even by day: the white door of Mrs. Haitch's shop. Anne wanted to find it. She wasn't sure if the magic would be there, for Mrs. Haitch had said it wasn't true; but the shop was full of strangeness and unwasting, that much at least was true.

Because she was watching so carefully, it was she who saw, as they turned the second corner, a familiar figure passing under a streetlight ahead. She stopped, astonished.

"Dad! Oh *no!* How did he find the way?"

"He'll get pneumonia!" said James, unbelieving and staring.

Mrs. Haitch had stopped too. "Beside himself, poor man. See you take care of him. He's let you have a good breathing space, remember, upset or not."

"Us?" said Anne. "That was them."

Mrs. Haitch smiled and shook her head. "Go on with you, now. I'll watch you on your way."

They started off. Anne stopped to look back and wave, then ran to catch up with James.

"Hang on, James—listen! He'll be upset like she said, and no William. We'll just say . . . he's all right, we've found him . . . and a lady's keeping him in a cage for us till later. Now you mind—don't make him feel bad."

She was back in her own world, the elder, in charge and doing her best. The other world would take more thinking about, but at least some bits were true.

There was Dad, running now in a wobbly way, wrapped up in his heaviest coat: searching the streets for them when he should have been in bed. Just as Mrs. Haitch had known he would.

There was William, still lost in Eternity. Just as Ruby had said.

And Eternity was the end of the world, the here and now. Just as Cyril had said.